To my number-one fan, Tolly, and his little brother, Ivo
- GPJ

To Mum, Jackie and Andy, for all their
encouragement (and sense of the absurd)
- SM

STRIPES PUBLISHING
An imprint of the Little Tiger Group
1 The Coda Centre, 189 Munster Road,
London SW6 6AW

A paperback original
First published in Great Britain in 2017

Text copyright © Gareth P. Jones, 2017
Illustrations copyright © Steve May, 2017

ISBN: 978-1-84715-785-0

PET DEFENDERS

BEARDS FROM OUTER SPACE

GARETH P. JONES

ILLUSTRATED BY

STEVE MAY

stripes

PET DEFENDERS

Protecting those who protect us

Did you know that Earth is under constant alien attack?

Don't worry.

We are the Pet Defenders, a secret society of domestic animals. We are your dogs, cats, rabbits and rodents. While you are off at school or work or doing whatever it is you humans do, we are keeping the Earth safe.

We keep our work hidden because we know what humans are like. The first sight of a yellow-bellied three-armed Flobber-Dobber with an electrocuting bottom and you'll panic.

TOP SECRET

Before you know it, you'll have blown up the very planet we're trying to defend.

Just carry on as normal — stroke your cats, take your dogs for walks and clean out your hamster cages. Don't forget to feed us, but please … let *us* take care of the aliens.

Now that you know all this, we need you to forget it. Our specially trained seagulls will take care of that. Ah, here they are with the Forget-Me-Plop now…

SSSPLAT!

CHAPTER 1

*

BEARDS ARE THE FUTURE

It was early in the morning when the seagull arrived. The large bird pecked on the glass until Biskit crawled out of his dog basket and nudged the window open. The message played from the speaker on the seagull's leg. Agent Biskit was to report to Commander F's Hutch Quarters at once. Usually Biskit would have groaned and crawled back under his blanket but today he dived through the dog flap and raced across town. He was eager to prove to his grumpy white rabbit boss that he was better than his new cat partner Mitzy.

The streets of Nothington-on-Sea were still quiet so Biskit was able to take the most direct route without attracting any attention. When he reached the garden where Commander F's HQ was located, he squeezed his way under the fence only to find himself face to face with a tabby cat.

"Nice of you to join the party," said Mitzy.

Biskit growled. "Yeah, well, I was at home with my owner rather than—" He stopped himself.

"Rummaging through someone's bin?" Mitzy finished the sentence for him.

"I didn't say that."

"But you were going to. Look, I never asked to be out on the street. I never asked to lose my owner."

"You're not the only one to have lost someone," replied Biskit.

Mitzy's tone softened. "Listen, I'm sorry about Champ." Biskit had told her about how his previous partner had gone missing after falling into another dimension.

"He was a good dog," said Biskit quietly. "And a good partner."

"I can be that, too — if you let me," said Mitzy. "Well, obviously not a dog…"

"You're not a bad agent but sooner or later you'll slip up, get hurt or drop out. Then I'll be on my own again," said Biskit. "It's better that way."

Mitzy knew Biskit blamed himself for his partner's disappearance. She felt bad for him – she really did – but she also knew he had to move on.

"Where is Commander F anyway?" she asked. "He's not in his hutch."

"Fluffikins is around here somewhere," said Biskit, sniffing the air to catch the rabbit's scent.

"Ahem."

They both turned to see a scowling face sticking out of a flap in the back door.

"Hi, Commander. I didn't see you there," said Biskit.

"Get inside. Both of you," barked the rabbit. "Now! And careful with this flap. It's pretty snappy. Oh, and wipe your paws on the mat for a change." His head disappeared back through the flap.

"Is he ever in a good mood?" asked Mitzy.

"Oh yes," said Biskit quietly. "I arrived early once and caught Emily tickling his ears. I swear I saw him actually chuckle."

"I can't imagine that," Mitzy said.

"It was weird," admitted Biskit, with a shiver.

Mitzy followed him into the house. Commander F was right about the flap. It snapped shut so suddenly that Mitzy lost a few hairs from the end of her tail. They headed into the living room where Commander F was sitting in front of the television. It was on but the picture was paused. It looked like the local news. Along the bottom of the screen was the headline:

FANCY-DRESS "KING" TIPPED TO BE NEW MAYOR

A man with a scraggly grey beard stood in front of an orange bus with loudspeakers on top and the slogan VOTE KING! printed on the side. He was bald and wore a pair of dark sunglasses.

"You need to watch this," said Commander F.

"The news?" asked Biskit. "I suppose I could do with some more sleep."

"Biskit, me old duck-worrier," said Commander F, "you might only watch silly films but as your commander I watch human news to keep an eye out for alien activity."

"What's unusual about this old beardy running for mayor?" asked Biskit.

"Watch," said Commander F.

He pressed a button on the remote control and a news reporter said, "Bradley Edwards was previously unknown in politics. He's the owner of a fancy-dress shop who has changed his surname to King and decided to run for mayor of Nothington-on-Sea. In a short time, he has picked up quite a remarkable following."

The television showed two men handing out bottles of brown liquid to a crowd of people. One of the men had a bushy ginger beard. The other had a neatly trimmed goatee. Both wore sunglasses. A close-up revealed the label on the bottle. It read: *KING COLA*.

"Handing out bottles of his cola has won over many hearts. Not to mention chins," continued the reporter, "and with the voting now over, tomorrow morning King looks set to become the mayor of this charming, if unimportant, seaside town."

The screen changed to show the reporter standing in front of the man called King, holding a microphone up to his bearded chin.

"Mr King," she said.

"King," replied the man in a deep voice. "We are just King."

"OK. Just King." The reporter raised an eyebrow at the camera as if to say *I've got a right one here*. "What will you do once you're mayor?"

"We will rule," he replied, looking straight at the camera.

"OK," said the reporter, still sounding amused. "And why is it that all your supporters grow beards?"

King's thick beard hid his smile as he replied, "Beards are the future."

"And he's not the only one who thinks that," said the reporter, with a wink. The camera zoomed out to reveal a crowd of people standing around them. They were all men and they all wore sunglasses and had beards. The overall effect was strangely spooky, especially when Commander F paused the television.

The Pet Defenders peered at the screen.

"Why do they all look like that?" asked Biskit.

Commander F growled. He was one of the few rabbits Biskit knew whose growl was louder and more threatening than that of most dogs. "That, my old marrow-munching mate, is what I need you two to find out. There's something very odd going on here. Our chief scientist, Example One, and his lab mice have reported a high chance of alien involvement.

It's your job to find out why all these male humans are suddenly growing beards and putting on sunglasses? What's in that cola that's being handed out? What does this King really want? That news report was broadcast last night—"

"Last night?" interrupted Biskit.

Commander F harrumphed. "Unlike you dogs, rabbits aren't exactly invited in to watch the television every night," he said. "Maybe if you showed more interest in the news than in that silly cartoon, *Danger Dog*, we'd have known about this earlier."

"*Danger Dog* isn't a cartoon. He's played by a real dog," said Biskit. "Several dogs actually. They're up to their third one now and—"

"I don't care," yelled Commander F. "You need to find King and, if he *is* up to no good, send him packing before ten o'clock this morning."

"Why? What happens at ten?" asked Biskit.

"He's due to be sworn in as mayor outside the town hall."

Before Biskit could reply, Mitzy said, "You can rely on us, sir."

"And try keeping this one quiet, will you? Example One is still restocking supplies of Forget-Me-Plop after your last little outing."

"Oh, excuse us for saving the world from a rubbish-eating beetle," said Biskit sarcastically.

"Saving the world is one part of the job," said Commander F. "Keeping your actions a secret is the other."

CHAPTER 2

KINGS AND CONQUERORS

As the sun rose over Nothington-on-Sea, the streets filled with office workers in suits marching to the train station and parents hurrying their children to school. Mitzy and Biskit stuck to the backstreets.

"The only fancy-dress shop in Nothington is Kings and Conquerors on the high street," said Biskit as they crept past a bus stop. "Philip took me there a couple of weeks ago. He was looking for a costume for a party."

"Was that his nephew's birthday? When he went as Dorothy from *The Wizard of Oz* and

made you go as her dog, Toto, in a pink bow?" said Mitzy, trying not to smirk.

"How do you know about that?" demanded Biskit, dropping his tail between his legs in embarrassment.

"I'm a Pet Defender agent. It's my job to know what happens in this town," Mitzy replied with a shrug. "Anyway, I didn't know Toto even had a pink bow…"

"He didn't," snarled Biskit. "Come on."

Kings and Conquerors was located between a barber's and a takeaway pizza place. Biskit and Mitzy hid under a bench across the road, unseen by the passing shoppers. There was a closed sign on the shop door.

"There's a window round the side," said Mitzy. "We can use that. Follow me."

She began to move but Biskit put a paw on her tail. "Listen, I'm the senior agent," he said. "You follow me, not the other way round."

"Fine," sighed Mitzy. "So what should we do?"

"We'll use the window round the side," said Biskit.

Mitzy smiled, checked the coast was clear then darted across the road. Biskit followed her into the alley. She hopped up on to a bin under a small open window at the back of the shop. Biskit jumped up, too, causing the bin to rattle.

"How did you know about the window?" asked Biskit.

Mitzy didn't reply – but as Biskit breathed in the smell of pizza, he knew the answer. Takeaway bins made for good scavenging.

They peered in through the grubby window. There were Roman centurion helmets, horned Viking hats and suits of armour. Some items hung from the walls, others were piled up in suitcases. In the middle of the jumble of clothing and props was King, snoring in a chair.

"What are you waiting for?" asked Biskit.

"We can't just rush in," said Mitzy. "We'll wake him."

"Not if we're quiet," said Biskit. "Follow my lead." He jumped up and wriggled through the window, pawing at the frame and pulling himself inside. He dropped down with a **CLA-DUMP** on to an old trunk.

Mitzy held her breath as the man twitched in his sleep then settled and began snoring.

"HORRCH-PISHH!-HERCH-ZZzzZ!"

Mitzy scrambled up on to the ledge then dropped down through the window, landing quietly next to Biskit.

"Let's take a look around," said Biskit.

"What are we looking for?" asked Mitzy.

"Something alieny."

"It all looks pretty normal to me," said Mitzy, looking up at a cowboy outfit complete with gun belt. The sleeping man was slumped on an armchair in front of an Attila the Hun outfit and a Henry VIII costume.

Biskit sniffed his feet.

"What are you doing?" whispered Mitzy.

"This nose remembers the scent of every alien I've met," said Biskit.

"And?" said Mitzy. "How does he smell?"

"Like someone who needs to change his socks." Biskit moved away from King.

"Come on," said Mitzy, "we need to ge—"

Suddenly the shop bell rang with a shrill

TRIIING!

King awoke with a start.

"HORRCH-PISHH!-Brrzz-"

Biskit dived into a box of medals and rosettes. Mitzy slipped under a large purple top hat.

"Ginger, Goatee, where have you been?" asked King.

Mitzy peeped out from under the hat while Biskit watched from the box as the two men from the news report stepped into the shop.

"Were you sleeping?" said the one with the ginger beard.

"Of course not," replied King. "I've been waiting for you two fools."

"Sorry," said the one with the goatee beard, "but we were trying to park the bus and I had to find change for the parking meter."

King stood up. "We care not for parking meters."

"Yeah, but the bus is parked on a single yellow," said Goatee. "And I wasn't sure how long you'd be. You see, you can only park for twenty minutes on a single line on a Sat—"

"Silence," cried King. "Bring the royal carriage to the door."

"Er, you mean the bus?" said Ginger.

"Yes, the bus! Bring the bus here."

"But this is a no-stopping zone," said Goatee, shocked by the very idea.

"Do not speak to me of such unimportant things when we stand on the brink of victory," proclaimed King.

"What are we standing on?" asked Ginger.

"The brink of something," said Goatee.

"It means that the first stage of our plan is almost complete," said King.

"How many stages are there?" asked

Goatee. "Because I've only put enough money in the meter for half an hour."

"Stop talking about parking!" yelled King. "Just bring forth the bus."

"You mean the royal carriage?" said Ginger.

"Just GO! Both of you. I will be out presently."

Ginger and Goatee hurried out. Alone in the shop, King spoke in a low, determined voice. "This time, my people, we will achieve our goal. This planet shall be ours."

Biskit was watching intently, peering out of his hiding place. Whether or not he was an alien, there was no doubt this King fellow was up to something. Biskit was considering jumping out and challenging him when a remarkable thing happened. The man's beard jumped off his face.

CHAPTER 3

THE BEARD KING

King's body fell back into the armchair, while his scraggly beard unhooked its hairy hands from behind his ears, swung its legs out from under his chin then clambered down his body. With its long arms and short legs, the beard lolloped across the shop like a small orangutan. It stopped by a large plastic container full of murky brown liquid.

The beard placed a tiny palm on to the clear plastic and spoke.

"Soon, my loyal subjects. Soon you will be needed to help lead us to victory."

The human on the chair stirred. His arm twitched, knocking his sunglasses to the floor. They landed in front of the purple top hat. Mitzy ducked out of sight but she was too late. The beard's tiny brown eyes of knotted hair spotted the movement.

"Reveal yourself, intruder, and bow before your king," cried the beard.

Mitzy pushed off the hat. "We're the Pet Defenders," she said. "We don't bow."

Biskit climbed out of his box. "But we have been known to bite," he added.

"And it is our job to get in the way of hostile aliens," said Mitzy.

The beard guffawed. "You clearly have no idea who you are dealing with."

Biskit and Mitzy looked at each other. "Why? Who are you?" asked Biskit.

"We are the Beard King," replied the creature, puffing out its hairy chest.

"Why do you keep saying we?" asked Biskit.

"It is the royal we," said the Beard King. "And we arrived on this planet long before either of you two did."

"What does that mean?" asked Mitzy.

"It means that this is not our first attempt at taking control of your planet but this time victory will be ours. Now, step aside, puny pets."

"You'll soon find out how puny we are," Biskit said. He sprang up and grabbed the strange hairy creature between his teeth.

"You fool," cried the creature. "You think you can trap me?" The beard's hairs slipped through the gaps in Biskit's teeth. "You will regret this treason."

"And you'll regret messing with us," said Mitzy. She pounced but it was like fighting a ball of extremely strong and rather wriggly string. Two hairs entwined themselves around her neck and dragged her off her feet and across the room. Biskit ran to help her but the Beard King caught him with a hair lasso then sent him skidding into Mitzy.

While they struggled to untangle themselves, the Beard King sprang back on to the man's chin.

As soon as the beard was back in place, the man bent down and lifted the plastic container. He smiled. Or rather, his beard smiled. When the Beard King spoke, he moved the man's mouth so it looked like the human was talking.

"We are leaving now. Our royal carriage awaits."

The orange campaign bus arrived outside. Mitzy and Biskit ran to the front door and blocked the way.

"This is where we cut you down to size, Beard King," said Biskit.

"Oh no," said the Beard King. "This is where we cut and run. I have a victory speech to make."

The Beard King bowled the plastic container straight at them. Mitzy and Biskit dived for cover and the container hit the door, knocking it wide open and rolling into the street.

A split second later, Mitzy and Biskit were back on their feet but the Beard King had already left and the door slammed shut in their faces. Mitzy jumped up and latched her mouth around the handle while Biskit shouldered the door. By the time they tumbled into the street the Beard King, the plastic container and the bus had disappeared around the corner.

CHAPTER 4

A HAIRY MOB

Mitzy and Biskit were about to chase after the mayor's bus when a seagull swooped down, surprising a postman who was walking along and whistling to himself.

"Hey! Watch it, you crazy bird!" said the postman.

The seagull landed in front of the Pet Defenders and then hopped into an alleyway. Biskit and Mitzy followed. When they were out of sight, Commander F's voice crackled out of the speaker. "Pet Defenders, what the crusty carrot is going on? This King fellow is about to be made mayor. What have you found out?"

"The human is under the control of his beard," said Mitzy.

"His beard?" exploded Commander F. Biskit could well imagine the carrot dropping from his mouth and the redness of his cheeks showing through his white fur. "What the soggy sprout does that mean?"

"He calls himself the Beard King," said Mitzy. "He appears to be an alien who came to Earth some time ago."

"Are you sure? I've never heard of him. What's he like, this Beard King?"

"Beardy," said Biskit.

"And crazy," added Mitzy.

"And what does he want?" demanded Commander F.

"Oh, the usual… Just to take over the world," replied Biskit casually.

"Take over the world?" Commander F exclaimed furiously. "So why the putrid parsnip did you let him get away?" The speaker crackled as Commander F raised his voice.

"We might have caught up with him if you hadn't stopped us," said Biskit.

"I don't want any public chases," said Commander F. "Besides, you had better find out what you're catching first. Go and talk to Barb before you do anything else."

"But sir," protested Biskit. "We know he's going to the town hall. If we head there right now, we can stop him becoming mayor."

"No," replied Commander F. "There will be too many witnesses at the town hall for you to do anything."

"But—"

"Agent Biskit," interrupted the grumpy white rabbit. "I am ordering you to go and see the fish immediately. Since you seem to have a problem with following orders, I'm making Mitzy the senior agent on this mission."

"Mitzy?" Biskit barked.

"Me?" said Mitzy.

The seagull flew up to a window ledge. "Yes, Senior Agent Mitzy," came the commander's voice. "I'm relying on you. Find out what we're dealing with. No heroics. No silly business. And no car chases."

"But sir—" began Biskit.

"I don't want to hear it. Just do your job."

The seagull flapped its wings and flew away, up and over the rooftops.

"So I suppose you're going to say we have to do as we're told and waste time going to see the fish," said Biskit, with a petulant wag of his tail.

"No." Mitzy stuck a leg in the air and cleaned her fur with her tongue.

"I hate it when you do that," said Biskit.

"I'm thinking," replied Mitzy. "We do need

to keep a close eye on the Beard King but Commander F is right. We need to find out what we're up against, too. I'll go and see Barb. You keep an eye on the Beard King. You'd better keep your head down, though. You heard the commander – no nonsense."

"Yes, Senior Agent Mitzy," said Biskit sarcastically.

Nothington town hall was a red-brick building, three storeys high that stood in a large paved square with a couple of trees, a few benches and a fountain with a statue of a young boy peeing into a pool of water.

A crowd of around a hundred humans had gathered to hear their new mayor's speech. Biskit crossed the road at the lights then slipped silently into the crowd. Some of the humans held placards or waved flags that read:

KING FOR MAYOR. Biskit made his way towards the mayor's campaign bus. It was parked on double yellow lines outside the town hall. The Beard King stood in front of the bus, addressing the crowd through a microphone.

"Thank you. Thank you," he said, waiting for the applause to die down.

"Friends, followers … follicles," he began grandly. "Lend us your chins."

"MAYOR KING ... MAYOR KING!" chanted the crowd.

"This town has voted us mayor but you, our most loyal subjects, know we are more than that. We are your king!"

"KING KING ... KING KING!" cried the crowd, raising their fists.

"You, our loyal subjects, have secured this town but, as you know, this is just the beginning. We are the few but soon we will be the many," continued the Beard King. "We will make this world our own."

"He does make a good speech," Biskit heard someone in the crowd saying.

"Yes, it's very rousing," replied another.

Biskit noticed that they both had beards and sunglasses. In fact, so did everyone in the crowd, including the women.

"We need your help," cried the Beard King. "Enemies are among us. Find the pets. Bring them to me."

Every human head looked down, searching

for the pets. Biskit felt hundreds of twitching
hairy eyes staring at him.

"I don't think he's talking about me," he said.

Had they been human they would only
have heard a barking dog but it was clear from
the eager twitching of the beards that they
understood every word.

"Get him!" cried the Beard King.

The bearded mob reached down to grab
Biskit but he dodged the clasping fingers. As he
zigzagged through legs, the Beard King's voice
echoed around the square. "Catch the dog.
Hold him."

Hands snatched, swiped and grabbed at Biskit as he ran. For each pair of hands he escaped, another awaited him. Deep in the frantic scrum, Biskit was wriggling and snapping his way through when he heard the hiss of the bus door.

"Soon we will be unstoppable," cried the Beard King. "Goatee, Ginger, it is time to take our royal carriage and complete stage two of the plan."

"Oh good," said Goatee, "because we're parked on double yellows here."

"Silence," cried the Beard King.

Biskit emerged from the crowd in time to see the Beard King, Ginger and Goatee step inside the bus, which immediately pulled away.

Commander F had quite clearly said *no more car chases*.

But that isn't a car, thought Biskit. *It's a bus! And I'm not going to let it get away again.*

Head down, legs like pistons, Biskit ran after
the bus.

BEEP! SCREEECH! HOOOONK!

Cars slammed on their brakes to avoid him
but Biskit ignored them. With a desperate
burst of energy he jumped on to the back
bumper of the bus, biting down on the licence
plate to hold on.

BEEEEEEPP!

Biskit looked back at the mob of bearded
humans standing on the pavement as the bus
drove away.

CHAPTER 5

❖

MORE COD
THAN GOD

Nothington-on-Sea's vet was a nice woman
called Dr Udall. She was polite, good at her job
and totally unaware that the goldfish she kept
at her surgery was in fact a super-intelligent
alien called Barb.

The vet's first appointment wasn't until
ten o'clock so Mitzy went round the side of
the surgery where a window looked in on
the empty room. Mitzy nudged the window
but it was locked. She could see the goldfish
swimming around its bowl. Mitzy tapped the
window and Barb turned, then flapped a fin.

The window instantly opened and Mitzy slipped inside.

"How did you do that?" Mitzy asked.

"I simply imagined the window open and it was," said a low female voice, as round and smooth as the bowl from which it came.

"You imagined it open?" said Mitzy disbelievingly.

Barb swished her tail and swam straight up and out of the bowl. As she drifted up, the water remained around her in a swirling globe. Mitzy had met Barb before but it was still an incredible sight to behold.

"Your problem," said Barb, "is that you see me as a fish but this is simply how I choose to appear in your drab little dimension. I have existed for many years in many worlds and in many forms. In some parts of the universe I am considered a god."

"But here you're more cod than god," said Mitzy, licking her lips despite herself.

"I can see spending all that time with Biskit is rubbing off on you," said Barb. "Speaking of which, where is he?"

"There's an alien in town calling himself the Beard King." Mitzy sprang up on to the vet's desk so she could look down on the floating fish.

"The Beard King?" repeated Barb, with a wry smile. "Oh, he's up to his tricks again, is he?"

"You know about him?"

Barb drifted up to Mitzy's level.

"Yes. The Beard King brought his people here many centuries ago from the swamp planet of Pogo located in the sixteenth hexagon of the seventh dimension," said Barb, as casually if she was giving directions to the local supermarket. "He was looking to expand his empire but their ship crashed and they've been stuck on your planet ever since."

"He was using a human body," said Mitzy.

"I understand the beards live in water on their home planet but here they can control other life forms by attaching themselves to their chins."

"He said he had tried before," said Mitzy.

"Many times…" As Barb spoke the room darkened and Mitzy saw an image appear in the air. She saw a young man wearing animal skins. The man bent down by a river to drink. Something leaped out of the water. The man covered his face with his hands then removed them to reveal a beard on his chin.

"Is that him?" asked Mitzy.

"Yes. Atilla the Hun, he called himself then," continued Barb. The image faded and was replaced with one of a fat king sitting on a throne. "Henry the VIII was another of his disguises. And there have been so many more. Name any bearded king or conqueror and there is every chance he was being controlled by his beard."

In the middle of the room, Mitzy watched images of men throughout the ages with various types of facial hair, leading armies, shouting commands and delivering speeches.

Barb swam around in a circle, wiping away all the images. "It has been many years since he last appeared. So which powerful position has he set his sights on this time? An army commander? Prime Minister? One of the judges on that celebrity dancing show that Dr Udall is always talking about?"

"He's just been made mayor of Nothington."

Barb laughed. "He is getting less ambitious in his old age." She blew a bubble, which travelled through the surrounding water then popped when it reached the edge, splashing Mitzy. She jumped back and sent a pencil flying off the desk.

"It's only a bit of water," said Barb.

Mitzy jumped down to the floor. "Why aren't you taking this seriously?" she asked.

Barb sighed. "Humans are always trying to seize power. What difference does it make if, from time to time, those humans are being controlled by beards from outer space. Now, you had better go." Barb drifted back to her bowl and poured herself back in with a **SPLOSH!**

Outside, they could hear Dr Udall saying good morning to the receptionist. Mitzy jumped on to the windowsill. "But you haven't told me how we stop him."

Barb did a flouncy little wiggle and said, "I have travelled to the remotest corners of this universe. I have witnessed many powerful kings intent on expanding their kingdoms. In the end it is always the same thing that stops them."

"What?" asked Mitzy.

She could hear the rattle of the key in the lock.

"Kings care more about themselves than their subjects," said Barb. "Now, please leave. It's ten o'clock."

The door opened and Mitzy dived out of the window, which slammed shut behind her. She was about to head towards the town hall to find Biskit when a seagull landed in front of her.

Commander F's voice crackled from its leg. "Agent Mitzy, my gulls are reporting that Biskit has just been spotted escaping an angry mob, then chasing after a bus in broad daylight. What the blazing beetroot is going on?"

"I'm not sure, sir. We split up," said Mitzy.

The seagull pecked the ground, showing no interest in the conversation between the cat and the voice coming out of the speaker on its leg. "So Biskit ignored my orders, did he?" demanded Commander F.

"No, sir, it was my idea but it doesn't matter."

"Doesn't matter?" Commander F's voice sounded distorted through the speaker. "Doesn't matter?"

"I don't know how the Beard King plans to

take over the world," said Mitzy as calmly as she could manage, "but he's tried it before and we need to stop him. Do you have any idea where the bus was heading?"

"Our seagulls tell me it's heading out of town on the northern road," said Commander F. "What I'd like you to do is—"

"Sorry, sir," Mitzy interrupted. "I have to go."

"Go? Where?" blustered Commander F.

"To help my partner." Mitzy sprang into action and the seagull leaped up in fright. She could hear Commander F yelling from the speaker but there was no time to waste. She had to catch up with Biskit.

Mitzy ran through a couple of gardens then up on to a high brick wall. She jumped down to a patch of wasteland by a high wire fence where a sign read CAUTION: LIVE TRACK. DANGER OF DEATH. Mitzy wriggled under the fence then looked both ways along the tracks. Using the bridge would take too long. She had to go over the tracks. There was a green light to the right but a red one to the left. A train was approaching, snaking round the corner, moving fast.

Deadly sparks flew up from the live rail. They reminded her of the time Biskit had almost died while saving the planet. He had never thought twice about putting his life on the line. This was no time for Mitzy to worry about danger.

As she jumped up and over the tracks, a **ZIIIINNNNNG!** rang along the rails and the ground shook. Mitzy moved fast, holding her tail high as she jumped each rail. The train **THUNDERED** and **RUMBLED** and **CHUGGED** towards her. Mitzy dived over the final rail and landed into a forwards roll, springing back to her feet as the train whizzed past.

CHAPTER 6

·🐾·

BOTTLED BEARDS

Biskit had been a thrill seeker ever since the day he had hidden in the washing machine as a pup, hoping Philip wouldn't notice him and turn it on. He never did find out what it felt like to go round and round inside the washing machine. Philip had spotted him, pulled him out and yelled at him so much that he never tried it again.

Biskit loved the excitement of his job so he was disappointed by how slowly the bus crawled through the traffic out of town. When it stopped at a set of traffic lights, Goatee hopped out to read a parking meter. Seeing his opportunity, Biskit snuck into the bus.

"Goatee, you fool," he heard the Beard King shout from the passenger seat. "Get back in here at once."

"Yeah, come on, the light's about to change," said Ginger, who was driving.

"Sorry. Coming," said Goatee. "I was just interested to see how much parking costs in this part of town."

"Idiot," snarled the Beard King.

As Goatee jumped back on board, Biskit took cover behind a pile of placards. Goatee passed through the bus then sat down at the front with the Beard King and Ginger. Biskit crept further inside, until he reached a crate of cola bottles that rattled as the bus trundled along. Next to them was the large plastic container of brown liquid. Biskit sniffed at it.

"Cola," he muttered. "What do they want with all this cola?"

He remembered how the Beard King had spoken to it back at the fancy-dress shop.

"Now, are you sure there's parking by the reservoir?" said Goatee.

"Stop talking about parking," ordered the Beard King. "Soon this entire town will be in our control, then we can move on to the final stage of our plan."

"Where we go back home?" asked Ginger.

"Home?" said the Beard King. "Once we

have conquered Planet Earth,
this will be our home."

"I miss Pogo," said Ginger, with a sad sigh.

"Me, too," said Goatee.

"Silence, both of you," cried the Beard King, "or I shall have you sealed in bottles for good."

Sealed in bottles, thought Biskit. He looked at the rattling crate of cola bottles. He peered right into one of them but the tinted glass made it impossible to see anything. He turned his attention to the plastic container. It was dark and murky inside but as he continued to stare he realized what he was looking at. The liquid wasn't cloudy. It was full of small hairy creatures. He caught a glimpse of a pair of knotted brown eyes looking back at him. Then another. "Beards," he gasped. "The beards are inside the cola."

Biskit spent the rest of the journey watching the beards swishing around inside the large container. Goatee had mentioned the reservoir, but why? Biskit was still trying to work out what it all meant when the bus stopped. He heard pop music playing outside. He peeked through the window and saw a security cabin. The guard turned the radio down and stepped outside.

"You're not allowed in here," he said. "This is a restricted area."

Ginger opened the window and replied, "We are here with the new mayor for his official inspection."

"An inspection? No one informed me. I'd better check with my boss."

"Yes, you could do that," said the Beard

King. "Then your boss will check with his boss, who will check with the council, who will check with the mayor … who is currently talking to you."

The security guard removed his hat and scratched his head. "Oh, your mayorship… I mean, your mayorness… I mean, mayoralty?" he stammered.

"King will do," said the Beard King. "Now, stop wasting our time and raise this barrier."

"Yes, Mayor King," said the security guard.

"King. Just King."

"Oh, right. Yes, Mayor Just King."

"Hmm. You look thirsty. Goatee, get this man a bottle of cola."

"Could I just ask about the parking situation—"

"Now!" yelled the Beard King.

"Right you are."

Biskit ducked behind a placard as Goatee plucked a bottle of cola from the crate and handed it to the security guard.

"It's my own special recipe," said the Beard King. "It's bound to put hairs on your chin."

"I think you mean chest," said Ginger. "The expression is put hairs on your... Oh, I get it."

"Er, I don't usually drink cola," said the security guard. "It's a bit sweet for my liking."

"I think you'll find this one *grows* on you," said the Beard King with a sinister chuckle.

The sound of the revving engine hid the laughter of the three beards as they drove towards the reservoir.

CHAPTER 7

CAT SPLASH!

Unlike her partner, Mitzy did not enjoy putting herself in danger but sometimes her job required it. After the near miss on the train track, she reached the northern road where she climbed an overhanging tree. She waited until a suitably sized delivery truck passed underneath then dropped down on top, sinking her claws into the roof.

It was a cold, terrifying way to travel and Mitzy was relived when she spotted the mayor's distinctive orange bus turning off the road. The truck driver showed no signs of slowing so Mitzy took a deep breath then dived into what she hoped was a big soft mulberry bush.

"WEOOW–" CRA-SMUNCH!

The mulberry bush was not as soft as she had hoped. Its thorns dug into her skin and its branches snapped under her weight, but it had cushioned the fall enough to avoid any breakages. Mitzy crawled out of the bush in time to see the mayor's bus driving through the open barrier. As she snuck past the security cabin, she glanced in to see the guard reading a newspaper with the radio on. On the desk was a bottle of King Cola. Mitzy continued into the reservoir where she found the bus parked across two spaces. Mitzy slipped underneath it. The door hissed open and a pair of feet appeared. The Beard King carried a large plastic container up the slope that surrounded the enormous manmade lake.

Mitzy was about to follow when Biskit stepped out of the bus.

"Biskit," she whispered.

"Mitzy," he replied. "We have to stop them. The beards are in the cola."

"The cola?" repeated Mitzy. "Barb did say they lived in liquid on their home planet. So what is he doing at a reservoir that supplies the town with wa—" Mitzy stopped mid-sentence. Her eyes widened. "Biskit, he's going to contaminate the water with beards…"

"Putting a beard on the face of every man, woman and child in Nothington," exclaimed Biskit. "We have to stop him!"

The Pet Defenders darted out from under the bus but two pairs of strong arms grabbed them and dragged them off their feet. They realized too late that Ginger and Goatee had been waiting for them to emerge.

"Aha! The boss was right. We were being followed," said Ginger, grabbing Biskit.

"Hey boss, we've got them," said Goatee.

At the top of the grassy slope, the Beard King turned around and smiled. "Ha, if it isn't those pesky Pet Defenders."

"You'll regret this," snarled Biskit. He bit down hard on the hand holding him but Ginger's grip remained tight.

"Unfortunately, hurting our human hosts has no effect on us," said the Beard King.

"That's good to know," said Mitzy. She reached a claw and yanked the end of Goatee's beard.

"YEAOOOUCH!" he cried, releasing Mitzy.

She dropped to the ground.

"Get her, you fool," cried the Beard King.

Ginger brought his foot down on Mitzy's tail causing her to screech.

While he was distracted by the sound, Biskit wriggled free. He barged into Ginger's leg, releasing Mitzy's tail from beneath his foot.

With Ginger and Goatee close behind, the Pet Defenders made for the Beard King but he was already at the water's edge, with the plastic container under one arm. As he unscrewed the lid and tipped the contents in, Mitzy jumped up, aiming to knock him off course and stop the liquid falling into the water. But the Beard

King grabbed her by the scruff of the neck and swung her round, whacking Biskit in the face and sending him tumbling backwards.

"You will regret your interference," the Beard King proclaimed, dangling Mitzy over the water.

Mitzy squirmed and wriggled to get free.

"Not afraid of water, are you?" said the Beard King.

The Beard King released her. Mitzy clawed at his arm but

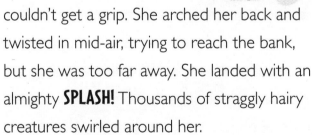

couldn't get a grip. She arched her back and twisted in mid-air, trying to reach the bank, but she was too far away. She landed with an almighty **SPLASH!** Thousands of straggly hairy creatures swirled around her.

If only I'd learned to swim, Mitzy thought.

CHAPTER 8

BAD SONG, GOOD CATCH

Mitzy tried to keep her head above the water, but no matter how hard she paddled she only sank further down. She waved her legs frantically but soon discovered there was a reason it was called doggy paddle. Cats didn't swim. Realizing there was nothing she could do Mitzy felt strangely at peace. She gazed helplessly at the beards swirling around her like hairy jellyfish performing an underwater ballet.

Then the spell was broken by a sudden **WOOSH**. Biskit latched his mouth on to Mitzy's ear and dragged her up through the water. He paddled hard, against the current of beards, which were spiralling deeper and deeper.

They broke the surface with an almighty **SPLA-DASH!** Biskit dragged Mitzy to a ladder and they both climbed out of the reservoir then collapsed by the water's edge.

"Thank you," said Mitzy, gasping for breath.

"Any time." Biskit stood up and shook the water from his fur.

"The beards are in the water," said Mitzy. "We failed."

"Not yet we haven't," said Biskit. "Come on."

Mitzy followed Biskit's gaze and saw the bus driving out of the compound. The security guard gave Goatee a cheery wave and went back into his cabin. Biskit set off down the slope after them but Mitzy stayed where she was.

"No," she said firmly.

Biskit paused. "What do you mean, *no?*" he said.

"We can't fight King and his beards without

fighting the humans we're trying to protect," said Mitzy. "We need to be smart."

"But…" Biskit ran around in a circle, desperate to chase after the bus. "You're saying we just let him get away?"

"He's already got away and the beards are in the water supply." Mitzy rolled over and dried her wet fur on the grass. "It won't be long before hundreds of beards are leaping out of taps and taking control of every human in Nothington."

"Which is why we need to go after them," Biskit barked in frustration.

"Our best chance of defeating them is to find a way of separating the beards from the humans," explained Mitzy patiently. "And that means getting a sample beard to the lab."

"There's no time for that! We need to catch the Beard King," exclaimed Biskit.

"We're Pet Defenders but we can't defend anyone if we have no way of beating these beards."

"You don't need to tell me how to do my job," said Biskit. "I was defending the Earth when you were still playing with balls of wool."

"Biskit, you're a brilliant agent—" began Mitzy.

"Thanks," interrupted Biskit.

Mitzy gave him a look and continued, "But you don't have to do everything on your own."

"It seems like I do actually," said Biskit, before adding with a defiant snarl, "Senior agent or not, I'm doing this my way."

He turned and ran.

"Biskit!" Mitzy cried after him as he raced past the security cabin and out of the compound. Then she remembered the bottle of King Cola in the security guard's cabin. As long as the man hadn't opened it yet, Mitzy could get the beard inside the bottle to the lab, where Example One would be able to work out a way of defeating them.

Mitzy snuck down to the security cabin and poked her head inside. The security guard had his feet up on the desk, and was reading a newspaper. The unopened bottle of cola was on the end of the desk, near his boots. The radio was playing a song she recognized. The man sang along tunelessly. "Yeah, yeah, yeah... Stick your hands in the air, air, air."

Mitzy looked up at the cola bottle. It wobbled precariously as the security guard's large feet tapped to the beat.

"Yeah, yeah, yeah. Like you just don't care, care, care," he sang.

Mitzy smiled at the thought of what her owner, Cynthia, would have said about the song. Cynthia hated pop music. Mitzy actually quite liked this song, although not as much as the security guard seemed to.

"Yeah, yeah, yeah. Why d'you stop and stare, stare, stare?"

As the thumping beat got louder the security guard's feet tapped more vigorously. Everything on the desk wobbled. The bottle of cola teetered on the edge. Mitzy crept into position, directly underneath.

"Yeah, yeah, yeah. Where d'you put your bear, bear, bear?"

Mitzy wondered if the security guard was singing the right words. Not that it mattered. The beat quickened and the foot tapping increased. Finally, the cola toppled.

Mitzy leaped up and grabbed the neck of the bottle in her mouth, twisting round and cushioning its fall with her belly.

"Stop right there…"

Mitzy froze, fearing she had been spotted until the security guard continued, "… there, there."

He was still singing along.

Unseen by the security guard, Mitzy took the bottle and ran.

CHAPTER 9

DOG ON A WIRE

It wasn't until Biskit reached the parade of shops on the outskirts of town that he spied his first beard. A mother with a pushchair stepped out of a newsagent's. She was wearing sunglasses, and had long black hair and a matching shiny black beard. Biskit ducked behind a bench, then watched through the slats as the mother and child approached. Her daughter couldn't have been more than two years old but she also had a neat beard on her chin.

Once they had passed, Biskit continued

through town. Everywhere he looked, he saw more unusual facial hair. A teenage boy on a bicycle with a large handlebar moustache, a lollipop lady helping children across the road with a beard so long, the end of it wrapped around her lollipop stick, a frail old lady with a long grey beard drooping right down into her shopping bags. Policemen with big bushy beards, joggers tripping over their long beards, young girls with pretty dresses and dinky little moustaches. The beard people were taking over and it was down to Biskit to stop them.

Mitzy was a good agent, Biskit thought, but she was too much like his previous partner, Champ. She stuck to the rules. She did what she was told. Champ had followed orders right up until the moment he fell into another dimension. After Champ disappeared, Biskit had decided to do things his own way.

Biskit reached an alley round the back of a block of flats across the square from the town hall. The streets were full of beards. Biskit knew his best chance of getting near the Beard King was to use the rooftops. He hopped on to a skip then sprang up on to a metal fire escape. On his way up to the roof he passed windows looking in on flats. Normal people doing normal things unaware of the danger all around them. Biskit caught a glimpse of a human sitting on a sofa with a Labrador pup lolling on his lap. For a moment Biskit wished he was back in his flat watching television with Philip. Then he noticed the man's big bushy beard. Biskit hurried on up the metal steps.

At the top, he moved to the edge of the roof and looked down. The whole building was surrounded by bearded people. Looking down at the streets, Biskit could see more of them swarming towards the square.

A voice came from the microphone in front of the town hall. "Gather round, gather round. The Beard King will be addressing you shortly." It was Ginger.

"Hopefully not too long," Goatee added, "we really shouldn't be parked here at all."

The microphone cut out and the beards continued to swarm towards the square. Biskit knew he had to get to the Beard King before he had a chance to give orders to his army.

Biskit looked warily at a telephone wire that ran between the roof he was standing on and the town hall. If he could get to the other end he would be able to drop down on to the bus. He prodded the wire with his paw. It wobbled. He had no idea whether it would hold his weight but there was only one way to find out.

He flung his paws around it and swung upside down, then shuffled along with all four

paws hooked around the wire. It shook
with the strain but Biskit kept moving as
quickly as he could towards the town hall,
unseen by the bearded folk below.

He felt the blood rush to his head. The wire dug into his skin and he tried to ignore the pins and needles in his paws. He had got halfway when he heard the snap.

The wire gave way. Biskit yelped as he dropped down and landed with a **SPLASH** in the fountain.

Every beard in the square turned to stare, fixing their small beady eyes on him. Biskit could feel water splattering on his head. He looked up. It was the statue of the boy peeing. Too late, Biskit spotted a brown hairy object shoot out of the statue towards his chin. He dropped and rolled, trying to tear it off but the small hairy creature had a firm grip. Biskit could feel a tingling sensation. He tried to scratch it but it just got worse. It was spreading. As the itching increased Biskit felt himself drifting away.

"My name is Biskit," he muttered. "I am an agent of the Pet Defenders…"

The sensation was too strong.

"My name is Biskit. I am an agent of the… My name is… My…"

The itching on his chin vanished. He closed

his eyes and gave in to the beard taking control of his body. He could hear a voice coming from his mouth but it wasn't his.

"This is your beard speaking. You are under my control now. We are loyal to our king, the Beard King."

CHAPTER 10

EXAMPLE'S SCARECROW

The Nothington Extra-terrestrial Research Division (or NERD, for short) was located in a secret lab where human scientists had once experimented on the mice that now worked there. The most intelligent of these was a pink mouse called Example One.

Mitzy approached a boarded-up door with the words KEEP OUT: DANGEROUS STRUCTURE written on it in red paint. She pushed one of the planks of wood aside and entered a brightly lit room full of beeping equipment, bubbling jars and cages containing all forms of odd alien objects. Example One scurried over to join her, with his electronic tablet under one arm. He adjusted his wire-rimmed spectacles and peered at the bottle. "Examples Five to Seven, carry this bottle to the Experiment Room. Be very careful not to drop it."

Three white mice approached. Mitzy heard her stomach growl and the mice froze to the spot, looking extremely nervous. She released the bottle and said, "Don't worry, I'm no mouser."

The mice carried the bottle through a door and Mitzy followed Example One into another room with a desk in front of a large window. Example One ran up a table leg and Mitzy jumped up on to the desk. On top was a control panel with various switches, levers and dials labelled things like Temperature, Brightness and Radiation Levels.

"Welcome to our observation room, where we perform tests on alien life forms," said Example One. He tapped on the window. "This is a two-way mirror. It allows us to see our subjects. It is bulletproof and soundproof."

Mitzy noticed a large crack in the glass. "What did that, then?" she asked.

"Ah, yes, well. It turns out it's not Fluger-horned Hippoproof." Example One sighed.

Through the mirror, they could see the three mice were placing the bottle in front of a scarecrow with a large pumpkin for a head and leafy branches for arms.

"What's that?" asked Mitzy.

"That? That's MOMM."

"Whose mum?"

"What? Oh, I see. No. MOMM as in Mouse-made Organic Matter Man," said Example One.

"It looks like that old scarecrow from Clifftop Farm," said Mitzy.

Example One adjusted his glasses and tapped his stylus on his tablet. "Ah, yes, well, it was. But now it has a far more valuable use than frightening birds."

Two of the mice left the room but the third remained behind.

Example One leaned on one of the buttons and spoke into a microphone. "Example Five, please remove the top of the bottle, then leave the area immediately."

The white mouse climbed up the side of the bottle, prised off its top with his mouth then darted out of the lab. The bottle erupted. Out of the top shot a dripping-wet beard that immediately attached itself to the bottom of the scarecrow's pumpkin head.

"As you can see," said Example One, "these beard people will attach themselves to the closest and largest organic matter in the area. Usually that's the human opening the bottle but in this case, it's MOMM."

The freshly bearded scarecrow sprang to its feet and took a couple of shaky steps.

"How is that possible?" asked Mitzy.

"The beard is controlling it. Once these things get their roots into their hosts they take control of their bodies, even if they are mostly made of vegetables."

The scarecrow lumbered about until it staggered into a wall, snapping some of the smaller twigs attached to its arms and sending leaves fluttering to the ground.

"A human being would have been a more reliable host but Example Eight wasn't comfortable with us experimenting on humans," explained Example One.

He tugged a large lever that operated a long robotic arm holding a small spray can. He pointed the can at the bearded scarecrow. The lolloping scarecrow stopped and looked at it. The robotic arm squeezed the trigger and the can sprayed the pumpkin. The bearded vegetable recoiled but the beard remained attached.

"Interesting. The subject responds negatively to low acid levels but beard and host are still connected." Example One pressed a button on top of the lever and the robotic arm dropped the can then swung over to a shelf and picked up another.

"How long will this take?" asked Mitzy.

"I've no idea," said Example One. "It could be hours until we find the right combination of chemicals to remove the beard. More likely it will be days. Possibly weeks."

Mitzy turned to look at Example One. "Weeks!" she exclaimed. "We don't have that long. Beards are springing up all over town. We have to do something now."

"You can't rush science," said Example One.

"Biskit is on his own," said Mitzy. "I need to go and help him."

"It would be better to avoid the beards until we have a solution," warned the pink mouse.

"As I've explained, these beards will attach to any living form. If one picks your chin, you'll be helpless to resist it."

"I don't care about that," said Mitzy. "I've got to help Biskit."

CHAPTER 11

🐾

BISCUIT'S BEARD

Mitzy's route from the secret lab to the town hall took her past the block of flats where Philip and Biskit lived. It was an area she knew well. Over the past couple of weeks she had secretly followed them several times. Mitzy didn't think of it as spying. It wasn't as though she didn't trust Biskit. He was the most loyal dog she had ever met. Mitzy liked to watch them because it reminded her what it was like to have an owner. She missed that feeling.

Mitzy kept high and out of sight. She walked along walls, over garages and across rooftops.

The streets were full of bearded humans, all heading in the same direction. Mitzy reached the flat roof across the road from the town hall. She stood at the edge, watching the beards arriving but she couldn't see any sign of Biskit.

Hearing footsteps behind her she turned to see Biskit step on to the roof.

"Biskit." Mitzy sighed. "You scared me."

"Your dog friend's been bearded. You *should* be scared." His voice sounded different. Mitzy looked again and saw that his eyes were closed and his chin was covered in thick curly hair. Biskit was being controlled by a beard!

"Release my partner," Mitzy demanded.

The beard gave a sinister chuckle. "The king wants you," he said.

"King?" said Mitzy. "You mean the king that brought your people to this planet against your will?"

"The Beard King is our king," said the beard, although Mitzy detected a note of doubt in his voice.

"I'll bet you were happy before you came here, weren't you?"

"Beards happy on Pogo, yes," admitted the beard. "But orders must be followed."

"I know someone who would disagree with that," said Mitzy, hoping for a reaction from Biskit.

"We beards are loyal to our king," said the beard.

"I feel the same about my partner. Release him or else."

"I choose else," said the beard.

"All right."

Mitzy pounced. She sank her claws into the beard on Biskit's face. She tugged with all her strength but the beard had sunk its roots deep into Biskit's skin.

"You are only hurting your friend," said the beard. "Come and I will find beard for you, too."

"No. I'm a Pet Defender and this is my planet," said Mitzy. "And I don't like beards."

"In that case…"

The bearded Biskit jumped on Mitzy. She rolled out of the way but he caught her tail between his paws. Mitzy screeched and pulled it free but he tugged it back then closed his jaws around the scruff of her neck and dragged her towards the edge of the roof. Mitzy hissed and scratched but Biskit kept a firm grip.

Mitzy stopped struggling as he dangled her over the street below.

"I told you to be scared," the beard said in a menacing voice.

All Biskit had to do was let go and she would drop to the pavement three storeys below. She had heard of cats surviving similar falls but she had no desire to put it to the test. She braced herself but Biskit didn't let go.

"Drop her, dog," muttered the beard.

Biskit growled.

He was fighting back! No matter how deeply he was under the beard's control, a part of him was unwilling to drop his partner.

"Oh well," said the beard, swinging his hairy feet and whacking Mitzy in the head. Mitzy felt Biskit lose his grip. She flicked her tail and curled it around his leg. Biskit dug his heels in to prevent himself from falling and Mitzy hauled herself to safety, grabbing the guttering with the tips of her claws and scrambled back up on to the roof. Before the beard could react she ran to the fire escape, darted down the steps and dived through an open window.

CHAPTER 12

*

FOAM OF DOOM

Mitzy found herself in a bathroom. She brushed past a vase of flowers on the windowsill and leaped down on to the toilet seat. As she made for the door, she could hear Biskit racing down the metal steps of the fire escape.

She tried the door but her paws were unable to get a grip on the round handle. The only way out was the window she had just come through – but that would lead her straight into Biskit's path. Mitzy watched the outline of the bearded dog in the frosted glass.

"I come to get you," called the beard.

Mitzy wondered if there was some way she could pull the shower curtain off and use it to trap him. She jumped up and tugged at it but it was securely attached. She looked around for something she could use to fight back but all she could see were bottles of shampoo and shower gel. She jumped up on to the basin where she found a pot with toothbrushes and toothpaste. Then she noticed a can of shaving foam and a razor blade...

With a **CLATTER-TA-KRACK-SPLOSH!** Biskit jumped in through the window, knocking the vase off the shelf and landing in the toilet bowl. The vase hit the floor and shattered.

Bearded Biskit climbed out, dripping toilet water on the floor. He looked at Mitzy and smiled. "Now you will get a beard of your own."

"I'll never wear a beard," said Mitzy, edging towards the razor blade.

"Oh, you will. When I flush this toilet, one of my fellow beards will come for you."

Biskit jumped up and flushed the toilet as Mitzy lunged for the razor. But her front paw landed on a bar of soap and she slipped. Mitzy and the can of shaving foam tumbled off the basin. Mitzy heard the flush and, within seconds, a soggy beard peered over the rim of the toilet bowl and began crawling out.

"Ah, my friend is here. Now you will join the beard brigade," said Biskit's beard.

Mitzy sprang to her feet. She was cornered but she wasn't ready to give up without a fight. She stepped forwards, but as she did so, she accidentally kicked the shaving-foam can, sending it spinning against the wall. The nozzle broke off and white foam shot out all over her.

"Don't worry. It will not hurt," said Biskit's beard.

Mitzy pulled herself back, raising her tail and lowering her head. She pounced at the same moment as the beard. They collided in mid-air, sending bits of foam everywhere. Mitzy scratched wildly at her chin, but the beard had not attached itself. Instead it had dropped to the tiles and was writhing around making a high-pitched screech.

"Argh, the foam of doom," cried the beard.

"The what?" Mitzy was confused.

"It burns, it scratches, it bites, it scorches." The beard crawled back to the toilet and climbed into the bowl.

Bearded Biskit backed away, too, and quivered in fear.

"Foam of doom?" Mitzy looked at the can of shaving foam, quietly hissing as its white frothy contents spilled out. "The shaving foam," she said.

"Keep away from me," said Biskit's beard.

"Of course. The way to fight the beards is with shaving foam." Mitzy grabbed the can with her tail and flipped it over then aimed it at Biskit. As she waved the tin, white foam sprayed all over the beard.

With a scream of terror, the hairy creature pulled itself off Biskit's chin and dived head first into the toilet. Water splashed out as it frantically swam away.

Mitzy ran to the edge of the bowl and looked down but both beards had vanished around the U-bend. The shaving-foam can spluttered as it rolled into a corner, empty. She turned to Biskit whose eyes were finally open.

"Feeling better?" asked Mitzy.

"The beard," said Biskit hazily. "Its voice was in my head."

"Yes, so are you ready, then?"

"Ready for what?" asked Biskit.

"Ready to save the world, of course."

Biskit's head felt like it had been through three tumble driers and a food mixer. His chin felt lighter now, but there was no time for a slow recovery – Mitzy had already jumped up on to the windowsill and left the bathroom. Biskit followed her out to the fire escape. A seagull stood on the metal handrail.

"I thought I said to keep things quiet?" Commander F's voice crackled out of the speaker on the seagull's leg. "There are more beards in this town than at a meeting of Father Christmas lookalikes!"

"Beards," said Biskit, placing a paw to his chin. "Yes, I remember. I was under its control. I attacked you." He looked at Mitzy.

"I won't hold it against you," said Mitzy.

"At least we know how to stop them now."

"We do?" said Commander F. "I thought Example One was still working on a formula."

"It already exists," said Mitzy. "It's called shaving foam."

"Shaving foam?" cried Commander F. "Is this some kind of joke?"

"No. She's right," said Biskit. "It was made years ago to fight the beards."

"Made? Made by who?" asked Commander F. "How do you even know this?"

Biskit's eyes looked distant as he spoke. "I could see its thoughts while it had control of my body. That beard could remember every time it had tried and failed to take over the world. Whoever came up with shaving foam did it to stop the beard people."

"I'll get all squadrons armed," said Commander F. "We'll drop a load of shaving foam on the whole area then whitewash the humans with Forget-Me-Plop. You two had better take cover."

"I'm afraid we can't do that," said Biskit.

"I might have expected you to argue," said Commander F.

"Sorry, sir," said Biskit. "There's no time. We need to stop the Beard King now."

"Stop him from doing what?" asked Commander F. "What do you know?"

"The Beard King is going to bring the rest of his people here," said Biskit.

"How?" asked Mitzy. "Aren't they on a planet on the other side of the galaxy?"

"Yes. But he's found a portal between his planet and ours. If we don't stop him opening it, he'll have enough beard people to take control of every living creature on Earth. We have to go NOW!"

CHAPTER 13

PORTAL TO POGO

"What is a portal?" asked Mitzy as she followed Biskit down the fire escape.

"A kind of big swirly hole in space that allows aliens to step from one side of the universe to the other. They're dangerous. Trust me on this," said Biskit with a determined snarl.

"You've experienced one before?" asked Mitzy.

"Yes. Champ and I were investigating one when he slipped through. The last thing I saw of him was his tail falling into that swirling circle of colour."

"I'm so sorry," said Mitzy.

"He's out there," said Biskit. "Somewhere, he's out there."

"Biskit," said Mitzy, fixing him with her stare. "He could be anywhere."

Biskit stared back defiantly, then sighed and said, "We've got a job to do."

Mitzy and Biskit stepped out into the main square. It was full of people, all facing in the same direction, awaiting their orders. The Pet Defenders slipped stealthily through the forest of legs towards the mayor's bus.

As they passed they heard the beards talking.

"Here we go again, another day, another plan to take over the world," grumbled a bushy brown beard.

"Apparently it's different this time," said a blond pointy one.

"I heard he's opening a portal to Pogo," added a trim beard worn by an elderly lady.

"I miss Pogo," said a moustache.

"So we can go home?" asked a patchy beard on a small boy.

"I don't think that's his plan, no," said another.

The crowd fell silent when a voice boomed from a loud speaker. Biskit spotted the Beard King appear from the sunroof on top of the bus, ready to address the crowd through a microphone.

"Friends, followers, our future," cried the Beard King.

The crowd erupted into applause.

"BEARD KING ... BEARD KING," they chanted.

"This is it," continued the Beard King. "This is the moment when we open a doorway that will bring forth an army to conquer this planet for good. Behold, the portal to Pogo."

The crowd raised their arms as they cheered, blocking Biskit and Mitzy's view completely. The Pet Defenders ran through the crowd until they reached the wall around the fountain, allowing them to see clearly. The Beard King, Ginger and Goatee were standing on top of the bus. Except now, between them and the town hall, was a swirling circle of light. It was as though a rainbow had got caught in a whirlpool in space. Within the colours were specks of light that sparkled like stars.

"That's the portal," whispered Biskit.

He dived back into the crowd, bounding towards the bus. The beards were still muttering.

"So home is just through there," said a thick moustache with sideburns.

"It would be good to see the place after all

this time," added a wispy white beard.

The Beard King's voice was still booming from the speakers. "Beard people, I am your king," he cried.

"BEARD KING ... BEARD KING..." chanted the crowd obediently.

"We have waited all this time. Now, finally, this planet is ours for the taking. Beards, raise your chins and prepare for victory!"

Biskit and Mitzy reached the bus but there was no obvious way of getting up.

"We could cut the speakers," said Mitzy.

"It's too late for that," said Biskit. "Any second now, enough beards are going to come through that portal to take control of the entire planet. We have to get up there. Follow my lead."

Biskit clambered up a nearby policeman's broad back, ready to use his shoulders to springboard on to the top of the bus.

"Hey, what's going on?" cried the beard on the police officer's face.

Mitzy was close behind. She clawed her way up a road sweeper then leaped off his head. All around, beard people tried to catch hold of them. Both Pet Defenders avoided their clutches until Ginger reached down and grabbed Biskit's collar.

"Hello again," said Ginger.

Mitzy was knocked off target by a bearded baker brandishing a French stick and was helpless to prevent Goatee snatching her by the tail.

"You won't get away this time." Goatee held her at arm's length.

The Beard King turned to address the crowd. "Ah, my Pet Defender friends have decided to join us to witness how we will conquer this planet. Welcome to the end of the world as you know it."

Biskit struggled to free himself but Ginger had a firm grip.

"We know about the foam of doom," said Biskit. "We know how to stop you."

"Stop us?" said the Beard King. "There isn't enough foam in the world to stop the army we are about to bring forth."

Behind them, the portal glowed and swirled and sparkled. In front, the crowd shuffled restlessly as they waited to see what would happen next.

CHAPTER 14

BEARD STAMPEDE!

With Goatee still holding her upside down by her tail, Mitzy stared out at the countless bearded faces of the people of Nothington-on-Sea. Hundreds of tiny knotted brown eyes were fixed on them. It was a terrifying sight, but Mitzy realized she didn't feel scared. She had heard the beards in the crowd talking. She had witnessed their uncertainty. These were not mindless warriors – they were a loyal people following the instructions of their king.

Mitzy suddenly understood what she had to do.

"Biskit," she said. "I need to get that microphone."

Biskit didn't need telling twice. He reached up and tried to grab the ginger beard but he was too low down. He knew hurting the human would have no effect on the beard but he could still knock him off balance. Biskit swung his weight to the side, causing Ginger to stumble and loosen his grip. Biskit dropped down on to the bus roof and charged at the Beard King, snatching the microphone between his teeth and tossing it to Mitzy. She was still being held by the tail but she swung towards it and managed to grab the mic with her paws and hold it to her mouth.

"Beard people," she said. "Listen to me."

"How dare you address my people?" said the Beard King. He tried to grab the microphone but Biskit blocked his way with a low threatening growl.

"Don't you want to hear what she's got to say?" asked Biskit.

"No," said the Beard King.

"Well, I do."

"Beards," said Mitzy. Her voice echoed off the walls of the surrounding buildings. "You don't have to follow your king's orders," she said.

There was a moment of silence as the crowd took this in.

"But … but he's the king," shouted someone.

"That's right. The Beard King," said another.

"He calls himself the Beard King," said Mitzy, "but he's no different to you. He's just another beard. And yet he took you from your homeland many years ago. Even now, he has opened a portal, but instead of using it to take you home, he's using it to bring more of you here."

"Beards are loyal," cried the voice from the crowd.

"Then be loyal to yourselves!" said Mitzy. "Do what you know is right and return to your home planet."

"Enough of this," said the Beard King. He aimed a kick at Biskit and snatched the microphone from Mitzy's paws.

"Beards, Braids, Brothers," said the Beard King. "This is our moment of victory. Finally we will make this planet our new home."

"A new home?" said Ginger. "We have a home and it's through that portal."

"That's right," said Goatee, "a home where

we make our own parking rules."

"Silence, fools!" snapped the Beard King.

"You shouldn't speak to us like that."
Goatee released Mitzy. She dropped down on
to the roof of the bus.

"Yeah, it's mean," said Ginger.

Goatee turned to address the crowd.
"Fellow beards, our king is a bad king."

"BEARD KING ... BAD KING..." chanted the
crowd. **"BEARD KING ... BAD KING..."**

"How dare you challenge me?" cried the
Beard King. "I am your king."

"You're a rotten king," said Ginger. "You
always have been. Now, we're going home."

Ginger jumped off his human chin, climbed
on to the top of his head then jumped into the
portal and vanished.

Goatee was next. Before jumping in, he
turned to the Beard King and said, "Two hours,
I've been parked on a double yellow line now."

"This is treason," cried the Beard King.

"It's over," said Biskit.

"Yes, give up," added Mitzy.

"Never." The Beard King raised the microphone and addressed the crowd. "My people, you must do as I say."

"Why?" cried a voice from the crowd.

"Why?" replied the Beard King. "Because I am your—"

His final words were lost as a seagull swooped down and fired a stream of shaving foam over him. He screamed and dropped from his human's chin. More seagulls circled overhead but before they could swoop, every beard in the square jumped off its human face and made its way over the heads of the confused crowd. As they reached the bus they ignored the attempts of the Beard King to block their way, trampling over him in their desperation to reach the portal.

"Beard stampede," cried Biskit. "Take cover."

The Pet Defenders dropped down inside the bus through the sunroof as hundreds of beards scrambled up and over it, desperate to jump into the portal before it closed.

Once all the beards had vanished and the portal had fizzled away into thin air Mitzy looked out at all the humans awaking from their beard trances. The beardless mayor was lying on top of the bus.

"His beard may be gone," said Mitzy, "but his memory of all this won't disappear so easily."

"Oh yes, it will. It's white-out time," said Biskit.

CHAPTER 15

WHITE OUT

Mitzy had never seen anything like the mass white-out that followed. The sky darkened with the squadron of seagulls and a downpour of Forget-Me-Plop dropped on every human head in the area.

Once it was over, the Pet Defenders emerged from the bus.

The portal had gone. So had the Beard King.

"Do you think he went back with them?" asked Mitzy.

"Probably. It's not like he could take over the world without his people," said Biskit.

"How did he open the portal in the first place?"

"That is a very interesting question," squeaked Example One arriving on the back of a seagull fitted with a specially made harness. He pulled a chip from the saddlebag and tossed it for the seagull then lifted his tablet and began making notes with his stylus. "There is still a lot we don't know about portals."

"So it could reappear and let them come back?" said Mitzy.

"I suppose that is possible," said Example One. "Still, at least everything is as it should be for now."

"Back as it should be?" cried Commander F's voice from the seagull's leg. "Look at this mess."

Although all the beards had gone and the townsfolk's memories had been wiped, there was still the problem of hundreds of people

standing outside the town hall with no idea
how they got there.

"We have every agent in town coming here
to lead their owners back home but this is
going to take quite some explaining."

The humans who had been taken over by the Beard King were sitting down, looking dazed and covered in white sticky Forget-Me-Plop. Every so often one of them would try to get up only for a seagull to swoop down and splat them again.

"As you can see, some of these humans need to have more memory wiped than others," said Commander F. "We think that Mr Edwards here has been under the influence of the Beard King for years."

"Poor man," said Mitzy.

"Yes. It's a big fat dollop-hopping shambles," said Commander F.

"We did save the world, though," said Biskit.

"Well, yes, but…"

"And we did it by showing that not all orders should be followed," said Mitzy.

"I'm still not a happy bunny, Pet Defenders," said Commander F.

"Perhaps we should pay a visit to HQ and tickle his ears," whispered Mitzy.

"What was that?" demanded Commander F.

"Nothing," said Mitzy.

Example One turned to Biskit. "So while you were under the beard's spell, did you learn anything else about these people? It must have been fascinating."

"Fascinating is not the word I would use," said Biskit, "but yes, I did learn something."

"What?" asked Example One excitedly. "What did you learn?"

"I found out why Nothington was so important to him. It turns out this whole place is built in a weak point in the universe, making it much easier to open portals here than any other place on Earth."

"You could see all this inside the beard's mind?" said Mitzy.

"Yes," said Biskit.

"Well, that is interesting," said Example One. "It would explain why we are so prone to alien attacks."

"It doesn't matter whether or not we are more prone to attack," said Commander F, "so long as we are here to defend it."

Later that day, once the humans had found their way back to their homes, Mitzy was perched on a tree branch, settled in for the evening. It was a place she had sat before. It had a good view of the inside of Biskit and Philip's apartment. They were on the sofa watching the news on the television. Biskit had his head in Philip's lap and Philip was stroking him with one hand while eating crisps with the other. Occasionally Biskit would roll his head over and Philip would drop a handful into his mouth. The flickering blue light of the television lit up their faces. Mitzy was too far away to hear what the news was saying about the day's events but she had no doubt that Commander F would have fed the news agencies some explanation of what had happened.

The truth had to be hidden.

The Pet Defenders' aim wasn't just to defend the Earth against alien attack – it was to keep their owners safe and unaware of the danger they were in. Since Mitzy's owner, Cynthia, had gone missing, Mitzy didn't have anyone to protect. She didn't have a warm fire or a soft sofa but watching Biskit and Philip was a reminder of why the Pet Defenders did what they did. They were sworn to protect those who protected them. They did dangerous things, not for the thrill but so that owners and pets everywhere were free to sit on sofas, eating crisps, without a care in the world. That was a right worth defending.